LIGHTHOUSE IN THE MIST

A fictional memoir of New Petrograd

HEATHER J. GRAHAM DIANA VAN GEFFEN
LORETTA SCUTCHINGS

Art by Fish Tailed Goat

Assisted publication by Moonshell Books, Inc.

Lighthouse in the Mist / Heather J. Graham et al -- 1st ed.

Created with Vellum

INTRODUCTION

New Petrograd was a village on Canada's Pacific Northwest coast that was settled when its inhabitants fled the Russian Revolution of 1917. Meet Phil Filipov, the village's lighthouse keeper, who will introduce you to New Petrograd as he takes you around the village, sharing the warmth of his friends and their memories of the times in which they grew up.

Part of the story involves newcomers Marvin and June Palmer, who bought the old Pagodon house and retired from their busy lives in Vancouver—or so they say. Steve Philip and Mark Feodociv sailed in sometime later, but it wasn't long before they were immersed in the village's activities, with their own stories to add to the town's rich history.

Lighthouse in the Mist is not only a fictitious memoir. It's daily life on the edge of a continent. It's a charming romance. And it's something more.

ACKNOWLEDGMENTS

This book was inspired by the life of Russia's Grand Duchess Olga Alexandrovna Romanov and in particular the information found in this article about her maid smuggling Russian jewels into Canada:

https://www.thestar.com/news/gta/2014/11/25/shabby_toronto_
apartment_was_once_home_to_russias_grand_duchess_olga.h
tml

The people who worked on this book were Heather J. Graham, Loretta Scutchings and Diana Van Geffen. They would like to recognize the following:

Shannon Gibson, a recreation therapist at their long-term care facility, for her assistance and helpful comments, for acting as their scribe, and most of all, for calling us to task when we got too chatty.

Lisa Drummond for her help with Russian translations and highlights.

Deb Moore for providing support with draft edits.

Fish Tailed Goat for creating the fabulous cover image (www.fishtailedgoat.com).

Shelley Bates, who was so instrumental in helping with the publishing (www.moonshellbooks.com).

PRAISE

I absolutely loved the book *Lighthouse in the Mist: A Fictional Memoir of New Petrograd*! In their debut novel, Heather J. Graham, Loretta Scutchings, and Diana Van Geffen sweep you away to the intimate and charming village of New Petrograd. The characters are intriguing, robust and well developed; as you make your way through the book you truly feel like you are sitting around listening to stories with a group of old friends. The authors' deep commitment to research and historical accuracy helps to truly bring the village of New Petrograd to life. With dashes of romance, humor, history, mystery and much more, this wonderful book has something for everyone! A fabulous read!

—Jacqueline Swindells

Lighthouse in the Mist by Heather J. Graham, Loretta Scutchings and Diana Van Geffen is a book set in modern-day North America and is full of interesting characters whose lives are all linked together by their common love of their mother country, Russia. The characters will have you smiling and perhaps reflecting on your ancestral ties too. Pick up this book and join in an adventure with the locals in their much loved village!

—Lisa Drummond

I loved reading *Lighthouse in the Mist: A Fictional Memoir of New Petrograd.* This story follows the fascinating characters of New Petrograd as they go through their days entangled with one another against the memories of their parents' tales of their homeland of Russia. With a little bit of everything, this enrapturing small town tale leaves you wishing you were there with the characters as well as in Russia partaking of some delicious sounding delicacies!

—Kanika Bharthi

This story is a breath of fresh air. It's about a small, isolated community where the residents help and support each other. They are also welcoming and supportive to newcomers to their community. I really enjoyed it.

—Carol-Lyne Carter

I found reading *Lighthouse in the Mist: A Fictional Memoir of New Petrograd* made me smile and question as the story unfolded. I enjoyed reading this and I found it flowed very well. I found myself trying to pronounce words I had never known and chuckling when I tried. The suspense was to the very end. Great job!

—Lorna Hayes

FOREWORD

I am so proud of our Garrison Green residents Heather J. Graham, Loretta Scutchings and Diana Van Geffen, who have taken the time to write this book with such enthusiasm and meaning, bringing enjoyment and perhaps memories to many who are lucky to experience the reading of this book.

It took me back to where I felt that I gotten to know the many interesting characters. This book intrigued me to want to learn more on how they were still able to bring their heritage and adventure from their much-loved country that they had to leave behind. The food, bonus recipes, little businesses in New Petrograd, the long journey of settlers and suspense of a maid smuggling Russian jewels into Canada ... wow, the list goes on with the many interesting situations that the characters experienced. You could not help but feel part of the experience.

Margaret Brausse, Manager of Support Services, Garrison Green and Royal Park

PART ONE

Lighthouse in the Mist

CHAPTER ONE

New Petrograd

A mist quietly rolls across the ocean, bringing with it a new day in the sleepy little village of New Petrograd in the Pacific Northwest. It is often referred to as sleepy, as nothing ever really happens here. We don't even have a sheriff for our village but Bob, from the Borscht Kettle, can fill in if needed. Before I go much further, allow me to introduce myself. My name is Phil Filipov and I am the lighthouse keeper at New Petrograd.

From where I sit, drinking my morning coffee and looking across the water from the lighthouse, it looks like a beautiful spring day, and one that I always feel invites warmth to rush through my veins. I just love this view, so high in the sky, which allows me to witness the expanse of the surrounding ocean. Then I look below me at the village of New Petrograd.

New Petrograd was settled predominantly by Russian immigrants after the Russian Revolution of 1917. No one new has moved here in decades. I love the comfortable feeling of knowing all my neighbours. Fact is, many I have known from my childhood days growing up in this village. I often think of the carefree days when Bob, Frank, my brother Ron, and I raced across the lush fields. A lot of time has come and gone since then with the noisy years of raising a family, the quiet years of being empty nesters, and now soon we will be facing new changes—retirement.

But this year, 1984, the old Pagodon house was sold to a couple who moved into our small, dormant village. The chatter amongst the locals is that their names are Marvin and June Palmer, a recently retired couple. It seems like they were looking for a quiet place to spend their retirement years.

On a typical day, I've often noticed Marvin heading off early in the morning to the end of the pier with his fishing rod. Even on the warm spring rainy days, I have seen his form through the mist. There may be a few chum or Coho swimming by, but not much comes this close to shore. Unless you consider a bullhead a fish. The playful otter is what I see the most of, not that you'd want to catch one. Still, it's a great way to spend a morning, but perhaps someday I will have an opportunity to suggest that a trip to a nearby river might be more rewarding.

On the pleasant spring days, June often accompanies him and then heads up into the meadow. Her pleasure seems to be in gathering a colourful bouquet of the many wildflowers that adorn it. The verdant countryside is rich with foliage and the green rolling terrain is perfect for such a ramble. Throughout the season there will be the lovely pink flower of the salmonberry, as well as the Pacific bleeding heart, the English daisy or the flowering currant. The grassy patches are covered in the cheery bright yellow flower of the buttercup, mingled with clover. Of course, intermittently, there is often the sprinkling of a few dandelions. In summer and fall, more flowers spring up in those fields. Out in the grasslands, one often sees eagles soaring overhead and small woodland creatures such as deer. Even the black bear will sometimes pay a visit, as he especially likes New Petrograd's garbage dump.

I am drawn from my musings to attend to my duties as lighthouse keeper. I must get busy cleaning all the windows so I will have good visibility in every direction.

CHAPTER TWO

Church

It was a cool early Sunday morning and I woke up to the sounds of the church bells ringing. I noticed the townspeople all dressed up in their best Sunday attire and heading toward the modest chapel. The chapel also happens to be the schoolhouse and the village meeting place. I rushed to put on my best and only suit and hurried to join the others going to church. It's nice to say hello to my old friends and I also hope to meet the new folk.

I sat in my usual pew and surveyed the congregation. I felt a bit disappointed because I didn't see the new couple. The long service finally ended and I joined everyone in the churchyard to greet those I knew. Well, having lived in New Petrograd all my life, I guess that means everyone. Betty Yusporova approached me with a hug and asked if, per usual, I was coming to dinner. I confirmed that I would be there and inquired if their son and daughter-in-law were also planning on coming. I was very pleased when Betty answered me to say that Alex and Anna would be there. I made my way across the churchyard to where they were chatting with John and Katarina Molodtsov and shortly afterwards, we all headed to Frank and Betty's house. They run the local store, New Petrograd General. I spend a lot of time with them and I grew up next door to Frank. It's no surprise that he married Betty, as they were childhood sweethearts. Betty had prepared beef stroganoff for dinner, which is one of my favorites. After a nice leisurely meal, a pleasant visit with a few laughs and a catch-up of local gossip, I thanked my old friends and headed on my way.

It was such a lovely evening with a warm breeze coming off the ocean that, on a whim, I decided to see if Marg Rosnokova would like to go for a walk. I headed over to her house on 5th Street. She seemed a little surprised to see me at the door, but quickly recovered and in response to my question, replied that she would love to but had supper almost ready and asked if I would like to come in and join her instead. Having had one good meal today, I declined and headed back to the lighthouse to put my feet up and start reading *The Shadow Riders*. The evening passed quickly and I retired early hoping to get a good night's rest.

I woke up early Monday and looked across the cold grey expanse of the water. A boat appeared through the morning mist and pulled up to the dock. Two unshaven and unkempt men got off. It ran through my mind that they needed to see Paul Katovik, our local barber. Incidentally, Christella Katovik runs the beauty parlour, which is right next door. The men tied up the old craft and surveyed their surroundings. The taller of the two men leaned forward, said something to the other man and pointed towards town. The men then started walking up the pier towards the village.

My eyes lingered on them as they began meandering around the dusty streets of the village. I had to wonder where they came from and what their purpose was in coming here. I watched them until they went into the Borscht Kettle, our local food and drink establishment. I soon put them to the back of my mind and my focus was turned back to what was happening on the water. As ocean liners and cruise ships sailed past, there was enough activity to keep me attentive.

CHAPTER THREE

Lighthouse Keepers

There's not much action anymore at this lighthouse. In fact, the Coast Guard has begun to automate it. This sure has freed me from the dawn-to-dusk hours to which I've been so accustomed. I think of all the years when Millie and the girls were with me and how strapped I was to my job. However, I am enjoying this newfound freedom because it is helping me to ease into retirement.

My *dedushka* and *babushka*, Vasily and Tatyana Filipov, and my *rhoditeli*, Pyotr and Elena Filipov, were some of New Petrograd's founding fathers. *Babushka* often spoke of the turmoil in Mother Russia and how quickly their love grew for their new life in the Dominion of Canada. It was a hard life, struggling against Mother Nature's demands in so many ways, but most importantly, they felt safe.

My papa was married soon after arriving in New Petrograd to his sweetheart, Elena. They had planned on getting married in Mother Russia, but before the big day came, they chose to join some others who were fleeing the unrest around them. *Babushka* often said that they had to promise her maternal *babushka* that they would ensure my mama's safety and that Pyotr would be married to her soon after arriving in the new land. The wedding took place on a cold, miserable summer day because they had sent to Bella Coola for a priest and he arrived that afternoon.

She would often say, "Phil, you should have seen your mama on that day, she looked so radiant in the gown she brought with her from the homeland."

Father Longo, who married them, decided to stay and became a part of New Petrograd as its first priest. This caused quite a stir around the village—a Russian Orthodox congregation and an Italian Catholic priest.

My *dedushka* was the first lighthouse keeper and his vivid stories enticed me to follow in his footsteps. He used to speak of the need for this lighthouse. A few months after they had arrived, there was a devastating shipwreck just off the craggy point. A lighthouse quickly became one of New Petrograd's necessities. Many of the village men left each day to fish and the need to keep them safe was on everyone's minds. After all, the fishermen were bringing home food to feed the settlement. This meant that papa and other men had to be taken from their job of building the hamlet to erect a lighthouse. I have always felt a sense of pride in this lighthouse just knowing that my papa had a part in building it.

Sometimes over the years I have sat up here and reminisced about the stories that my *dedushka* would tell about those early days. How important it was to live in tune with the changing seasons. How proud he was of my *babushka* and my mama who laboured through much hardship to perform all their responsibilities with a song on their lips. He spoke about how the men folk cut the enormous Douglas fir trees and skidded them across land to build homes, the church and stores. And how slowly a way of life had emerged as the village of New Petrograd came to life. He would smile and tousle my hair and add that soon in every household could be heard the patter of little feet.

These recollections would always bring to mind the idealistic childhood that I shared with my siblings and friends. I could picture again the happy, carefree days that Bob, Frank, my brother Ron and I enjoyed, including the fun and the pranks we got up to. *Dedushka* loved to tell these stories. Particularly after *babushka* passed. She was the love of his life, and he was left lonely and isolated afterwards. I can also relate, now that my beloved Millie is gone.

As evening started to cloak the day into dusk, I decided to drop into the Borscht Kettle for supper. I was anxious to talk to Bob about the two men I saw sailing in this morning and had last seen entering his restaurant. My friends Bob and Olga are the owners of the Borscht Kettle. Olga Petrova is also the schoolteacher and so, during the school year, is rarely seen at the restaurant.

CHAPTER FOUR

The Borscht Kettle

"Gee, it's quiet in here," I greeted Bob as I came through the door.

Bartender Bob laughed and passed me a pint of my favorite drink, *kvass*.

"Much action on the water today, Phil?"

"Well, there was something. I saw two strangers dock their boat and start walking down Marine Street. In fact, I think the men came in here this morning."

"Yes," Bob agreed, and then silenced as the door opened and the two men walked into the room and sat at the other end of the bar.

"A couple of beers," one of them ordered as they sat down.

"I'll have an order of the daily special," I told Bob, before turning in my seat to greet the other customers. I had noticed that they were the new couple. I walked across the room to their table, extended my hand in greeting and said, "Hi, don't let me disturb your dinner, but I just wanted to take this opportunity to introduce myself. My name is Phil Filipov. I'm the lighthouse keeper here. I had heard that there were new owners of the Pagodon house and was anxious to meet you."

The man turned with a smile and said, "Pleased to meet you, Phil. I'm Marvin and this is my wife, June."

June interjected, "Pleased to meet you. Oh, it's so nice to get to know some people here."

"Where did you move from?" I asked.

"Vancouver—have you been there? It is so fast paced, we just retired, Marvin worked for TELUS and I was a trauma nurse. Boy, was that an exhausting job...." June rambled on.

I must say that I really wasn't sorry when Bob brought out my meal.

I finished the conversation by saying, "Nice to meet you. Welcome to New Petrograd."

"Thank you," they both chimed.

"Do you know anyone who needs renovation work done around here?" the taller of the two strangers spoke up and asked Bob.

"Well," Bob started to say, when I heard the high-pitched voice of June exclaim, "Yes, we need some work done at our house."

Both men turned their heads to look at her, and the taller man said, "Great!" as he walked over to their table. But he paused first, and then asked, "Boy, does that ever smell great. What is it called?"

"Cool something," Marvin started to say.

Bob responded by saying, "They ordered the daily special. It is called *coulibiac*; it is a Russian dish. We start with fish, traditionally sturgeon, but salmon can also be used, and is what I used today. We make a loaf, and then add rice, hard-boiled eggs, mushrooms and dill."

"If it tastes anything like it sounds, I think I will have some as well."

"Steve, what about you? Should we make that two orders?" the taller man asked.

"Sure," his friend replied. "Can we get it to take out?"

Bob laughed and said, "Well, we don't really do take-out, but I'm sure I can arrange something."

Turning again after the brief interruption, the taller man put out his hand to Marvin and smiled at June.

"What did you have in mind? I am Mark and sitting over there is my friend, Steve."

"Pleased to meet you. My name is Marvin and this is my wife, June," Marvin responded. "You certainly can take a look at all the renovation projects we have in mind. Where are you staying in the village, so that we can get ahold of you?"

"We just sailed here this morning, but are planning on staying on our boat. It's docked at the harbour. How about we set up a time now to come and look at your projects and write up an estimate?"

"For sure, we are just up Marine Road in the house with the turret. It also has a large verandah in front—I'm sure you can't miss it. How about you come by tomorrow around noon?" Marvin replied while turning to June for confirmation. "Maybe bring along some references when you come."

"Oh gee," Steve said. "We sailed yesterday and then realized we hadn't brought any."

"Oh well," Marvin answered. "No problem you coming by tomorrow and having a look anyways."

Soon afterwards Marvin and June called out "good night" and left.

Steve and Mark went back to the bar to finish their drinks

and wait for their meals. I overheard them laughing and saying something about "what luck."

Suddenly the one called Steve swung himself around on the bar stool and asked, "Is there a barber here?"

To which I was only too happy to tell him the he could find a barber just a few doors down.

"Stick around and you will soon find everything here is just a few doors down," I chuckled to myself.

Soon afterwards Bob managed to get something together for their take-out and Mark and Steve said their good nights.

"I sure have a weird feeling about those two," I said.

"Oh," Bob replied, "I didn't get that feeling. They seem fine to me. Maybe need a little cleaning up, but other than that, both times they came in, they seemed polite and all."

"Well, I hope you're right. We don't need any trouble here," I replied. 'Well, Bob, I suppose I should say good night and head home as well. I started reading a good Louis L'Amour book last night and am looking forward to getting back to it."

As I stepped out into the evening, there was a brilliant golden sun just beginning to set. I always love watching this ball of gold sitting on the horizon before it slips into the sea. As I walked past Mark and Steve's boat, I noticed the lights were all turned off and everything seemed quiet.

CHAPTER FIVE

Quotes Galore

I woke up in the morning still in my easy chair and realized I must have fallen asleep last night while reading my book. I remember trying to set it down several times, but Dal and Mac Traven always seemed to call me back to the pages.

I moved to the kitchen in a bit of a stupor to make my morning coffee. Soon the invigorating aroma was tickling my senses. I poured myself a cup and stared out at the shore, where the waves were crashing against it. I was watching, but not really seeing, as my thoughts went back to the words I'd overheard Mark and Steve utter last night—"what luck." By mid-afternoon, when these words were still plaguing me, I decided to go for a walk to clear my head. Before I knew it, I found myself in the vacant field behind Marvin and June's place with no recollection of how I got there. I strolled through the long grass enjoying the fresh air, which helped to penetrate my foggy mind. I finally settled on the thought that Mark and Steve were probably just relieved to have found work. After all, who could blame them? They had only sailed in that morning.

I heard my name and looked up. Marvin was waving from his yard and as I came closer I saw that he was mowing his lawn. He stopped the mower and headed toward the fence. After we greeted each other, I asked him if Mark and Steve had come by today to look at the renovation jobs.

"Yes, they did!" Marvin responded. "They gave me an estimate but in Vancouver I usually got two or three estimates for comparison purposes. I really wish I could do that now."

"Well," I told him cheerfully, "it's not a problem to at least get one more quote. Tony Rosso is an excellent handyman here in the village. In fact, he and his wife Daria live just across the street. Would you like me to introduce you to him?"

"Sure, when?" Marvin replied.

"How about now? We can see if he's home," I said as Marvin opened the fence gate and we strolled toward the impeccably restored early century house.

I knocked on the door, and soon Tony answered it.

"Hi Tony. I'd like to introduce you to your new neighbor, Marvin Palmer," I said.

"Hello," Tony responded and shook hands with Marvin. "Please step inside. We knew the Pagodon house had recently sold. We saw you moving in and didn't want to get in the way, but we fully intended to drop by and introduce ourselves. Sure is nice to meet you. Welcome to New Petrograd."

"Thank you," Marvin answered. "Everyone has been so welcoming. We are very happy that we moved here."

"They are looking at having renovations done at their place. They got a quote this morning from two chaps who sailed into the village yesterday, but Marvin was just mentioning that he wishes he could get another one. I was pleased to tell him you do that kind of work."

"Well, you know," Tony laughed, "taking on another job might delay my retirement."

I laughed back and said, "Tony, you'll never retire. This village needs you too much."

Tony responded by informing me, "Oh, did you hear? Gaspar is coming home. He's had enough of big-city life. He is planning to take over my business. Daria is so excited that she doesn't know what she is doing most of the time."

"I do too," Daria called from the kitchen. "I'm making my boy his favourite dishes, Phil."

"That is fantastic news," I responded.

Daria poked her nose in long enough to welcome Marvin and to say she would be over soon to meet June. Marvin and Tony began to chat about the renovations and it was decided Tony would come by after supper to have a look.

The conversation ended so Marvin and I pleasantly said, "See you later," and we were on our way.

"Thanks, Phil," Marvin was saying as we crossed the street and came adjacent to his yard.

I noticed June was in their garden and when I called hello to her, she whipped her head up and looked like a she had just been caught. She fumbled over her shovel and it appeared that she was having trouble filling a hole she had dug.

"Here, let me help you," I said while I took a step toward her.

"No, no. I am just fine. Where have you and Marvin been?" she asked as she started moving towards the house.

"Phil took me across the street to meet some of our neighbours, Tony and Daria Rosso. Tony also does renovation work. He is coming by after supper to give us a quote."

"Oh great," June answered, "I'd best get supper on."

I chatted a few minutes longer with Marvin, and then continued my walk.

As I stepped inside the Borscht Kettle, I noted to Bob, "It sure looks quiet tonight," seeing that their only other customers were Paul and Christella, to whom I waved in greeting.

"Yes," Bob replied.

Olga stepped out from the kitchen, "Bob called me to keep him company so I told him that I don't mind if I do keep company with the man I married thirty years ago."

To which Bob shyly responded, "I know how tired she is when she comes home after a day of teaching, so I really hesitate before asking her to come here."

Changing the subject, I asked, "What's on the menu tonight?"

"Chicken Kiev," Olga answered.

"Sounds perfect, I'll have an order and a *stewle* to drink."

A little later in the evening, I found myself telling Bob and Olga about Gaspar coming home.

"I sure wish Mary Ellen would come back," I said. "Maybe she could take over teaching and let you retire, Olga."

"Well, that would sure be nice," Olga replied.

We chatted a bit longer while Bob was preparing to close for the night.

"Going home to read your book?" Bob asked.

"Nope, I finished it last night," I responded with a yawn.

"Just wondering, Phil," Olga asked. "Do you have the whole collection of Louis L'Amour books?"

"Nope," I answered her, with a smile. "But you are right; I do have enough to sink a lighthouse." Amidst their laughter, I left.

Before going to bed, I took a last look outside and the

lighthouse beam shone on June, out in her garden again. She was back at that same spot and then moved to another corner of the garden.

What could she possibly be doing in her yard this late at night? Her actions today sure puzzled me. I felt that I might have solved the mystery of what Mark and Steve meant about "what luck," only to replace it with the question, "Why is June acting so oddly?"

Soon afterwards, I put both of these questions out of my mind, crawled into bed and turned out the lights.

CHAPTER SIX

Fish and Chips

I have always been curious. I guess that's one of the reasons why working in a lighthouse, where I can see everything for miles on land and sea, has brought me a lot of satisfaction. I always enjoy watching the village children walking to school in the morning and skipping home at the end of the school day. Or the water gently lapping at the shoreline or ferociously attacking the coast. Or watching Uri Golubov, Bob and Olga's son-in-law, coming in safely from a day of fishing. It was also special to catch a glimpse of a doe in the meadow with her two spotted fawns wobbling along behind her.

The day passed swiftly enough, when towards evening I observed Marvin and June going into the Borscht Kettle. I hadn't spoken to them since I had introduced Marvin to Tony, so I was pleased that I was also planning to go there.

"Well, Bob," I noted as I stepped inside the Borscht Kettle, "it looks like the whole village is here tonight."

"Sure is," Bob replied. "You know the tradition that my *rhoditeli* started all those years ago of having fish and chips on Friday?"

"Yes," I replied, "it was a marvelous idea that Aunt Margarita and Uncle Nikolai had and I am so glad you've kept it up. It brings back such good memories of our childhood, doesn't it? With my order I also would like a glass of *stewle* and whatever you have for dessert."

Bob laughed in reply, "You know the traditions as well as I do. I had Frank order in several gallons of ice cream for tonight."

"Oh, make mine chocolate," I answered him with a wink. "Before I sit down, though, I'd like to chat a few minutes with Marvin and June."

"No problem. Just flag down one of my helpers when you're ready to eat, and they will bring your order to you. I saw the Palmers sitting over there by the front window. I think they've already learned to come early on Friday nights."

I made my way over to where Bob had pointed and asked if I could join them.

"Sure thing," Marvin replied, "We were hoping we would see you here tonight, and also Mark and Steve. We've been mulling things over for a week and have finally decided on who we've chosen to hire for the renovations."

"I think I just saw Mark coming through the door, but he looks to be alone," I responded as I waved him over to the table.

"Hi everybody," Mark said. "Good to see you all."

"Good to see you also," we jointly responded.

Marvin continued, "I was just telling Phil that June and I were hoping to see you here this evening. We've decided to give you boys the renovation job. Your quote was a lot more what we had anticipated paying."

"That's grand news; we sure appreciate it," Mark replied.

"Steve wasn't feeling well tonight, so he decided to stay on the boat, but he'll be thrilled when I tell him."

"Do you need to order some supplies or tools?" I asked hesitantly.

"Yes, we will. I have to admit that I was wondering about that. We may need a few days to sail somewhere to pick things up. Where do you suppose would be the closest place?"

"No need to worry. Frank can order in anything you need at his general store. How about you meet me at eight in the morning outside Petrograd General and I'll introduce you to Frank?" I offered.

"Tell me where we might find it and we'll be there," Mark answered me with a smile.

"It is just a couple of doors further on the boardwalk from the Borscht Kettle. Frank keeps good clear signage. You can't miss it." I added with a chuckle, "Not that you can miss anything in New Petrograd."

"I've been thinking," Marvin interjected. "Why don't we spend tomorrow fishing? You will be spending quite a bit of time in our home. This will give us an opportunity to get to spend some time together. That is, if Steve is feeling well enough."

"I like that idea. We could use our boat to sail somewhere," Mark commented.

June quickly spoke up, "I was just going to offer to bring you some lunch around noon. Of course, that will mean you have to stay on the shore."

Suddenly I realized how quiet June had been all evening. Maybe it had been the conversation, but it just didn't seem like her. Was there some other reason?

"Well, that's something to think about," Marvin turned to smile at his wife and said, "Both ideas sound appealing to me.

Maybe I'll meet you when you place your order in the morning and we can decide."

Just then, one of the students Bob had hired to help him tonight approached Mark with a ready-to-go meal. I had to smile when I realized that this take-out thing wasn't just a one-time incident. Mark quickly said good night and was leaving, with us all calling out to say hello to Steve.

June added, "I hope he feels better tomorrow."

I kept the smile on my face, though, when I saw Marg coming through the door. I excused myself from Marvin and June, and approached her to ask if she would care to share a table with me.

"This room is so crowded, I agree," Marg said. "Sharing a table would free up one for someone else. I see a table just became ready in that corner beside Uri and Anna."

So soon I found myself reveling in Marg's company.

There were so many butterflies flying around in my stomach that I barely heard her say, "I think it is great that Bob carries on our *rhoditeli's* tradition of serving fish and chips."

"I totally agree. I was just saying to Bob that it brings back such happy memories of when we were kids," I answered her. "Bob keeps the tradition, even down to ordering gallons of ice cream for dessert."

"Well, in that case," Marg responded in delight, "I want a whole gallon of strawberry for myself. Speaking of memories, do you remember the night the Molodtsov children got into a food fight?"

"I remember mostly the trouble they got into from their *rhoditeli* and then how on Monday at school we all had such a laugh."

Then, Marg was saying, "Then came all the years we would come as a family—Merle and me with the boys."

"I know Millie and the girls counted the days until the next fish and chips night. I have loved being a lighthouse keeper, but one thing I have always regretted was missing out on so many special occasions."

"Yes," Marg commented, "Millie and the girls often shared a table with us. It is five years now since I lost Merle. It was right around the same time that Don moved to Whitehorse to start a fishing and hunting outfitting business. Then shortly afterwards, Brad left for Toronto to attend university. So suddenly I was living by myself and I can't say that it's been all that great. Meal times, oh my, I sure am not good at cooking for one. I'm with your girls, Phil, counting the days until fish and chips night."

"Yes," I responded, "I remember what a shock to the village it was when Merle had his hunting accident."

I resisted the urge to take her hand and instead I simply said, "I know what you mean about being on your own. It's already been three years since I lost Millie to her illness. My twin baby girls had already moved to Vancouver. I have hopes Mary Ellen might move home to New Petrograd and take over being the schoolteacher so Olga can retire, but Marianne, she seems more intent on traveling the world. Tell me some about your boys, Marg. Are they married? Any grandchildren?"

"I'm very excited. Brad got married last year and now there is a baby on the way. I am ecstatic at the thought of being a grandmother, but I do feel the distance. I don't even feel I have a way to really get to know his wife, Cheryl. Of course, we speak on the phone and she seems so nice and very friendly, but it just doesn't seem the same as spending time with her. She has often commented that if I was closer we could spend a day shopping together at one of the many malls and I just laugh. The way she describes shopping seems a bit different than going to Frank and Betty's store and placing an order to come in on the barge. Don, well, I think he is like your Marianne, with no thought of settling down and plans to travel the world. Maybe they should have gotten married.

"Speaking of marriage," she shyly continued, "I know my *rhoditeli* used to tease me about us getting married."

"Mine too," I could barely whisper, while inside my heart did strange things.

Walking home later that evening, my head was exploding from the pleasant occurrences of the evening. How easily the conversation had flowed. We talked about so many things, from reminiscing about the past to sharing the present.

Marg even told me something that I didn't know. The idea of giving us children Canadian names had come from the district nurse, Miss Green. She had explained to our *rhoditeli* that this would help establish our families and us children in Canada. Marg was eager to learn about the automation of the lighthouse and my pending retirement.

Fish and chips night had never tasted better. Such thoughts sprinted through my head as I relived our conversation. The last thought I had before I drifted off to sleep was whether Marg had enjoyed the evening as much as I had.

CHAPTER SEVEN

Frank's General Store

Early in the morning I poured a cup of coffee, looked at the clock and realized that I had better hurry if I wanted to make my eight o'clock meeting with Mark and Steve. I must admit to myself that now that they had a chance to see our local barber, Paul, and were looking more presentable, I was finding I quite liked them. Bob was right when he spoke about how polite they were.

I had just stepped outside the lighthouse when I saw Mark and Steve moving off their boat. I hurried up and took a couple of long strides before I could call out a good morning. They both turned their heads and greeted me.

"How are you feeling?" I asked Steve as I joined up with them.

"Much better, thank you," he replied. "I'm not sure what happened; sometimes a migraine comes out of nowhere. I think the news Mark brought home last night had as much as anything else to do with me feeling better today. I couldn't even manage to eat the fish and chips."

"Well that is a shame; they were so good," I said, thinking

back over last evening. I pretended not to notice the strange look Mark and Steve gave me. *Who cares if a smile crossed my lips?* By the time we reached the general store, Marvin had met up with us and together we went inside.

Frank looked up as we came in. "Good morning," he greeted us. "I hope business stays this good all day."

"Good morning," we greeted him back.

I turned to the others and said, "Frank always was the class clown and his humour hasn't changed."

Frank responded, "What do you mean? Four people passed through my door and it's only eight o'clock. What's a businessman to think?"

Betty, rolling her eyes, looked at me from where she was busy stocking shelves. "You're right, Phil, he still is such a clown."

I quickly got busy introducing Mark and Steve to Frank and explained that they had an order to place for some materials.

Marvin added, "They are starting a renovation job at our house."

Marvin and I idly looked out the window. It really was a beautiful day. Puffy white clouds, all curvy like a woman, were floating across the endless blue sky. I couldn't help but think how delightful spring is with new life springing up all around us. Across the road, by the sea's edge, I saw the white flower of the Lady Finger unfolding. I especially always enjoy observing the trees shooting new green leaves. Standing in the General Store, I had time to observe all this—such simple details that I missed when looking down from the lighthouse.

Soon I heard Frank explaining, "I will need to order from different suppliers in Vancouver. Your order will arrive on a barge that comes weekly, so you will be able to pick up your items on the pier. An order this size will take at least a week, possibly even longer. Of course, that's depending on the weather, but usually in the spring it is good."

"Thank you for everything—ordering our supplies and the information about the barge," Mark said.

"Business all done, boys?" Marvin said. "Let's go fishing! I told June this morning that I like the idea of going out in your boat. I haven't had much luck from the pier, so getting out in deeper water might be the answer. June quickly put together a lunch that we can take with us. I heard her say something about sandwiches but I'm not sure what else she put in this cooler. I know I'm hoping she put in some chocolate chip cookies that she baked last night."

They walked me back to the corner where I wished them a good fishing trip, and then they set off for the pier where Mark and Steve's boat was anchored.

I had just finished my lunch of a hastily slapped together peanut butter and jam sandwich when I noticed June going into the Chrysalis hairdressing shop.

Around five, when I was quitting work for the day and setting up the automated system, I decided to get some exercise. As I walked past the beauty parlour, I could see June still in there. In fact, there seemed to be a whole bunch of women. I noticed several clusters of two or three, all quite engrossed in their conversations. In one corner Marg seemed to be very animated in the conversation she looked to be having with Betty and her daughter-in-law Anna.

My usual walking route continued to the old Pagodon house—uh, Palmer house. I noticed how attractive June's garden looked and it had a lot more plants. I thought she must enjoy more than wildflowers. This helped me to feel better about why she might be in her garden late at night.

I stopped to take a breather as well as take a huge gulp of all the lovely scents in the spring air. I was just contemplating whether some plants were vegetables or flowers when I heard my name called. I turned to see Daria working in her yard.

As I was crossing the street to say hello, she was saying, "Amazing garden June has. She spends so much of her time attending to it." She yanked a couple of weeds. "We really haven't done anything to welcome them. I'm thinking of doing something simple, like popping in one day with some baking."

"Daria, that sounds like a lovely idea," I agreed, before adding, "I was at the general store the other day and noticed Tony ordering a large supply of paint. I wonder if he plans on using it for the Founding Fathers' plaque?"

"Well, I don't know for sure," Daria replied, "but it would make sense because I know he always likes to get it painted and take care of any repairs it needs before Russia Day."

Soon I wished Daria a good day and continued on my way, past the row of cedar trees, and then circling back. I really had to think about Daria's comment. I'd shown Marvin and June friendliness, but maybe I should be doing more. I liked the idea of popping in for coffee one day.

The village women were so good at doing kind and thoughtful things. Leave it to us men and nothing would ever happen.

My route always brought me past the boarded-up old church. This was the church where Father Longo used to deliver his sermons. I can still hear his pleasant voice sharing the glories of heaven with us. Even as a child, I was spellbound by his stories.

I paused to read the inscription on the plaque in recognition of our founding fathers. It has always given me a thrill to see the names of my *rhoditeli* along with the names of my *dedushka* and *babushka* engraved on it.

There was another thing I could do—thank Tony for doing such a good job of keeping it painted and in good repair.

This plaque is in memory of the first settlers of New Petrograd who came to the Dominion of Canada after fleeing the Russian Revolution of 1917.

Pyotr Rosnokov and Nadeshda Rosnokova
Roman Molodtsov and Katerina Molodtsova
Pyotr Filipov and Elena Filipova
Vasily Filipov and Tatyana Filipova
Yaroslav Pagodonov and Tatyana Pagodonova
Alexander Yusporov and Anastasia Yusporova
Pavel Katovik and Yulia Katovik
Nikolai Petrov and Margarita Petrova
Mitslav Golubov and Olesia Golubova

FOUNDERS OF NEW PETROGRAD

CHAPTER EIGHT

Anna and New Petrograd History

The next day I seemed to be in a very peculiar mood. I kept thinking about what Marg had said about Miss Green, amongst other things she shared. It would be so nice to read something about New Petrograd's history.

These thoughts niggled at me all day while I worked and when I saw the schoolchildren leaving the schoolyard, I made up my mind to speak with Olga. I quickly turned on the automated system, thinking once again how wonderful it would have been to have had this switch when Millie and the twins were here. Then I hastened to the school hoping to catch Olga before she left for the day.

I wasted no time in asking her, "Are there any books on New Petrograd's history?"

"No, Phil, there aren't any books. New Petrograd just isn't that prominent a place," she playfully replied. "But speak to Anna Yusporova. She knows a huge amount of the village's history. She may even have some of it written down. You could invite her and Alex to come this evening. I am sure she could answer all your questions."

"That's a good idea, Olga. I think I will do that. What about you and Bob? Could you both come as well?"

"We just might be able to. Bob has been talking to Anna about working at the Borscht Kettle occasionally—you know, on quieter nights—to give him a night off. Secretly, I think he is trying to interest her in the business so he can retire."

So that is why later that evening I found myself hosting a coffee party for seven. I had also included Alex's *rhodeteli*, Frank and Betty, in my invitation.

But that wasn't what was special about the evening. Well, okay, I guess it was special because I can't recall doing something like that before but ... Anna reliving the stories of our founding fathers in her soft voice, making the story come alive ... telling of their trek across Mother Russia to England ... of the fears they faced each day ... how quiet they needed to keep as they trudged along. Eventually they made their way to London, where they boarded a steamer sailing across a massive body of water to a city called Halifax, where they first set foot on Canadian soil. She told of how, with tears in their eyes, they had bent to kiss the earth.

Anna paused there to say, "Can you just imagine how our *rhoditeli* felt about this new land that would soon become their home?"

I couldn't speak and my eyes had gotten misty, so I just nodded. I could hear sniffling from various spots in the room, and saw Olga get up to get a box of Kleenex to pass around.

Anna went on, "There they met Canada's immigration people, who told them of homesteading land in the west. So, they boarded a train and crossed this endless land to its other shore."

I asked, but even Anna didn't know how many days they were travelling at this point, but she suspected nearly a year.

"Their journey wasn't over yet, because when they again met with the authorities in Vancouver, they were awarded this portion of land up the coast. From Vancouver they continued, but this time they purchased a couple of fishing boats and sailed."

"Amazing they didn't capsize with so many in a boat," I muttered.

She concluded by saying, "And to think many of us are now a part of this history."

Much of what Anna had told us I already knew from my *dedushka* and *babushka*, but there were also interesting details that were new to me. Frank and Alex commented on some particulars Anna had shared that even he hadn't heard before.

Someone mentioned, "That is a lot of traveling. And buying fishing boats to sail up the coast—I wonder how they paid for it?"

But no one knew the answers. Alex did suggest that if his *dedushka* Yusporov had been here this evening, maybe he would know.

When Anna stopped talking, Olga piped up to remind us that soon we would have our annual Russia Day celebration observing Mother Russia.

"The children are so excited," she said, "planning on how they will decorate their bikes. With summer coming, it is so hard to get them to concentrate."

"I can relate," Anna commented. "I'm madly sewing for the traditional dress costume contest." We men just listened, except for Alex agreeing with Anna that it was difficult to get her to stop sewing long enough to make his supper.

Anna and Olga eagerly chattered away about their plans for Russia Day.

I broke in to ask, "Anna, do you think you could share the story then that you just shared with us here?"

"Now, that is a thought," Olga piped up to say. "It really would add a lot to Russia Day."

But then they went back to discussing the food they planned on bringing, which was of some interest to us, but I never got an answer to my question. Bob, Alex and I were soon standing at the windows looking at the very large sun melting into the blackened waters of the ocean. Bob, Frank and Alex were especially enjoying this exceptional view from my vantage point in the sky. We concluded this extraordinary evening indulging in the leftover pie and drinking the last of the coffee.

I said good night to my guests, feeling thankful the light from the shops would light their path partway home. But soon they would be going on the side streets, which were only lit by the moon. Some things in New Petrograd have never changed from when our founding fathers first arrived.

For the second time that week, I went to bed with my head whirling from the day's events.

CHAPTER NINE

Renovations Begin

I woke up in the morning to the low, eerie sound of an island barge coming towards land. Nothing like that eerie sound as an alarm clock, I thought, as I hurriedly threw on my shirt and jeans. Already I could see Frank with his hand-truck racing from the store along the pier to where Joe, the barge's captain, always docked.

New Petrograd is one of its many stops as it travels up and down the Pacific coast bringing the same pleasure to other little hamlets. As I made my way outside, I saw several of the village folk gathering along the pier.

I liked to tease Joe that he was one popular man, at which he would laugh uproariously and say, "That is what they say everywhere I dock."

Amidst all this flurry of activity, I saw Mark and Steve on their boat tentatively surveying the entire bustle. It seemed that in no time the crew had unloaded boxes of all sizes and shapes onto the pier. When I saw packages that looked like they might be flooring, I waved Mark and Steve over.

"It looks like this may be your lucky day," I said when they came closer.

"Oh man," Steve responded, "I am getting so tired of lying around reading books. It will be great to have a crowbar in my hands again."

"I second that," Mark added. "Put a crowbar or a mallet in my hands and I'm a happy man. There are just so many walks a guy can take around this village. Phil, do you have any suggestions on how we can move everything to Marvin and June's place?"

"Not a problem," Frank said, overhearing the conversation as he came alongside us. "I have some pretty big packages myself for stocking the store. I'm going to race home to get my truck to pick them up. Be back in a sec. I noticed a few of those boxes had your names on them, so maybe in the meantime you can put them all together."

"No problem," they both answered as they began to move towards the end of the pier.

I stood in my spot, quite enjoying observing the very familiar scene. Slowly the excitement of the morning was waning and it seemed like almost everyone in the village was leaving with a package or two. Bob was still at the end of the pier sorting through the remaining boxes when the boys came up to join him. I was just coming abreast of them when I heard Bob asking Joe if he had time for lunch.

"Well, Bob, me and the boys would never turn down one of your meals. I just need to take the mailbags to John at the post office. I usually take a minute to enjoy a coffee and chin-wag with him while I'm there. Often the crew comes into John's Kiosk as well, to stock up on a supply of chocolate bars, chips, magazines—I really don't know what all they waste their wages on. They say it takes away from the monotony of sailing and the long hours between hamlets. As for me," Joe added, "I'm content with the endless miles of ocean and space."

"You know the usual drill," Bob responded as he got into his vehicle. "Come when you're ready. Olga is always eager to hear what news I can tell her about your family."

"Same with Helga, as she is always eager to hear news of everyone that I visit with when I am away," Joe answered.

"Joe," I commented, "it's the same every week, a flurry of activity and then it's just you and me."

"And the mailbags," Joe ended.

Stooping to grab one, I chuckled at the weekly joke.

As we made our way across the pier, Joe asked, "Who were the two lads I noticed leaving with Frank?"

"We really don't know anything about them, other than their names. They just sailed in one morning in early spring. The taller one is Mark and his friend is Steve," I replied. "Remember me telling you about the couple who moved here who are doing some renovations at their house? With your cargo today were the supplies they had ordered—at least, some of them. So, this afternoon they should be able to start working. They seemed pretty excited at the prospect."

After helping Joe deliver the mailbags, I stayed long enough to enjoy a cup of coffee and a bit of a visit with John and Joe. I had just stepped outside when I saw Marg coming towards the post office.

I quickly cleared my throat, swallowed and barged into the speech I had been preparing in my mind. "Marg, how would you like to get together, you know, like at one of those school picnics?"

"Well hello to you too, Phil. How are you? But yes, it would be lovely to go on a picnic with you. I could ask my brother for —what did you say the boys called it?—a take-away."

Gathering my wits about me, I quickly replied, "Yes, that's what they called it. And I can bring something to drink. If four-thirty would be fine, I will come to your place."

"I will be ready then," she replied, and continued on into the post office, leaving me in wonder that she had actually said yes.

CHAPTER TEN

First Date

The day seemed to evaporate in a blur. The cuckoo clock on the wall ticked *Marg, Marg, Marg* all afternoon—or was it my heart beating? At four o'clock, I hastened to clean myself up. A flip of a switch to turn the automated system on, and I was off.

I think I walked from the lighthouse to Marg's place in a trance, because afterwards I really couldn't recall any of it. She was all ready to go with a picnic basket in hand, which I quickly relieved her of as we made our way to her garage where she still kept Merle's truck.

Marg was saying as we walked, "After your comment earlier today about school picnics, I wondered what you would think about driving over to the Rushing Falls. We could reminisce about how we used to walk over at the end of every school year. Remember how Tatyana Filipova used to say that it was a celebration that she had lasted another year."

"I used to think it was more of a celebration of my survival," I muttered, while turning to Marg to agree that it would be a perfect spot.

In truth, I really didn't care where we went, but it did seem like an ideal suggestion. It was a bit of a ways from New Petrograd, and yet not too far, which seemed just right.

"Growing up, I thought it was Russian Falls, not Rushing," I added, helping Marg to stow the picnic basket in the truck.

"Well," Marg commented, turning to me with a kind expression, "I can understand why you would think that. The words really do sound the same."

After helping Marg into the driver's side, I went around the vehicle checking the tires to be sure they could handle the rough roads we would be traveling over. It really wasn't my plan to have a flat tire, and all of New Petrograd in on our first date.

As we drove off on the bumpy road that cut through the bush, I relaxed enough to take notice of what a lovely evening it was. The temperature was so mild, with fluffy white clouds dancing across a clear blue sky and the spring smells of the surrounding foliage drifting through the open windows.

Suddenly Marg let out a little yelp.

I turned to see what was the matter, but she just pointed out the windshield and said, "Look, there's a deer with two fawns."

We stopped a few minutes to enjoy watching her bounce along with her babies close on her heels before they disappeared into the trees. Soon I was telling Marg about the doe and fawns I had observed from the lighthouse. It might even be the same deer.

Before long we had arrived at our old school picnic spot, and amidst the chatter of squirrels and chipmunks scolding us for invading their space, Marg deftly spread out a red and white tablecloth on the ground and set out the dishes. I added the apple juice I had brought, apologizing to Marg that I really thought I had some red wine.

Marg just laughed it off, exclaiming, "Phil, not to worry, I think this will be perfect."

She then quickly proceeded to unwrap a cut-up chicken from the aluminum foil Bob had put it in.

"Well now," I commented, 'if that isn't the perfect picnic food."

"I had my suspicion that is what he had given me," Marg commented. "Bob and Olga are always so concerned about my eating. It really doesn't surprise me; he probably thought he was giving me food for a few days."

"And here you are, sharing it with me," I remarked, looking in what I hoped was a questioning way.

Marg just kept on placing some salads, bread and pickles on the tablecloth and then finally she declared, "Ready to eat."

Together we uttered one of our childhood graces, and then Marg began serving me.

"Marg, Marg," I said like the cuckoo clock. "Serve yourself and then relax. I can help myself."

When I went to pick up a drumstick, and it looked like Marg was going for a wing, our hands briefly touched, and an electric shock went up my arm. Marg also looked like a lightning bolt had hit her.

When our plates were both full, we sat back leaning against a log, while the birds from the nearby pine tree serenaded us. When we finished eating, I stretched out against the log, listening to Marg put away the last of the food in the basket.

The next thing I knew was a peck on the cheek, and I looked up into Marg's smiling grey eyes looking down at me.

"You know, Phil," she murmured, "I went home Friday night and thought that fish and chips night never tasted better."

I sat up then with a jolt, as an electric shock went down the other arm, and replied, "But that's what I said."

She gave me such a look of surprise that I had to wonder if she had also felt another lightning bolt. Hastily getting up, I reached for her hand and we strolled together along the creek to stand and watch in awe, as we always had at Rushing Falls, with the water like a horse's tail racing to the rocks and ending in a spray. It was so pleasant as the two of us stood together listening to the thundering sound of the falls. The spray floated through the air and lit on our bare arms in a fine mist.

I had just taken a step closer to Marg to catch another whiff of her tantalizing perfume when she turned to me to say, "Look at the rainbow in the—" She got a splash on her nose, and then another one. "Phil, this isn't mist, it's raining."

Sure enough, when I looked up, I observed how the lovely, clear blue sky we'd had earlier had turned to grey and indeed rain was falling.

Turning back to Marg, I foolishly repeated what she had just said to me. "It's raining."

She looked at me and sighed. "Yes, I guess we had better go. We both know these Pacific Northwest weather patterns—it could rain for a few minutes or continue for days."

I took her arm so she wouldn't slip, and we hurriedly retraced our steps, skirting the puddles that were already forming, to pick up her picnic basket and then made a dash for the truck.

Walking back to the lighthouse after a nightcap at Marg's invitation, despite the rain still falling, the sun was shining inside me. Even Marg had said that it was a perfect evening.

While I was getting ready for bed, the cuckoo clock had changed its tune to *per-fect, per-fect, per-fect.* I think my last thought for the day was that a picnic had never tasted so good.

CHAPTER ELEVEN

Russia Day

It has long been a tradition at the end of the school year to have a celebration. We simply call it Russia Day, in remembrance of Mother Russia and our love for our founding fathers and mothers. I really am so fiercely proud of my Russian heritage. It has always been a day in the year that I have taken off. But first there was work to be done to set everything up, so I headed to the schoolyard to lend a hand.

When I arrived, several of the village men were already gathered.

"I think that there are two men here for every job," Tony chuckled. "There is a request for an additional table this year. After the contests, Anna Yusporova has offered to recite the history of New Petrograd. I think it will be a very fitting addition to our day. I am suggesting it be placed near where they set up the *zakuski*."

I turned to Bob with a nod and we set off to take care of this project, which set us up perfectly to help the men afterwards with the temporary kitchen. With so many men eager to help, Tony was right. We were finished so early that there was time for me to go home.

As I headed out, I met Marg. As soon as we got to the schoolyard, Marg headed off in the direction of the temporary kitchen. She said that she needed to drop off the *blini* she had brought for supper. I wandered the grounds and stopped to exchange a few pleasantries with several folks. I was watching the children getting ready for the bicycle contest when Bob came up behind me.

"Was that my sister, Margarita, I saw you walking with?"

"Yes, we met coming here," I responded, then turned away as I felt my face redden.

I had just noticed Marvin and June, so excusing myself from Bob, I hastened over to greet them.

"I am so glad to see you here. Someone must have told you about our celebration. I apologize—I should have done so myself."

"No need to apologize. I saw a poster at the Petrograd General Store and asked Betty about it," June responded.

Marvin joined in the conversation. "It seemed that it would be a good time for everyone. We decided to mention it to the boys. They decided to come as well." He pointed to the two empty chairs beside him.

Mark walked up just then, and added, "Marvin anticipated that it would be very busy, so he suggested setting up chairs early. He told us that it would be the last work we had to do for the day," he concluded with a smile towards Marvin.

"Well, most days they are hard at it, so we felt they deserved a break," Marvin offered.

"I hope you also anticipated a hat and suntan lotion. I think this afternoon is going to be a real scorcher. Some years we haven't been this lucky with the weather." And with a "See you later," I was off mingling with the crowd again.

Soon Martin Shatrov, who was acting as the emcee, picked up the microphone and welcomed us all to the 64th Annual Russia Day.

"I am so pleased to announce that Alexander Yusporov, our last remaining founding father, is well enough to join us today."

Amidst much clapping and cheering, he announced the first event of the day—the children's bike decorating contest.

"We need all the children to come forward with their bikes. Good luck to my Angela and everyone else," which brought much laughter.

Soon the cordoned-off area was filled with the children proudly showing off their bikes.

"Oh, I like Maria Katovik's bike," Marg said, as she came up alongside me.

When I looked up it seemed that, from every angle, everyone's eyes seemed to be watching us.

"I have to agree it does really stand out from the rest, but you know, I kind of like Peter Molodtsov's bike. It's big and bold."

We watched while the judges circled the contestants and then handed a piece of paper to Martin. Martin's next words came as a surprise to everyone.

"This year we've decided to do something different. We will give the children their prizes now. For the rest of you, your prizes will come at the end of the day, as usual." This brought murmurs of approval amidst laughter.

Martin then proceeded, "I must say that the judges had a hard time deciding, because everyone did a remarkable job. Children, you should all feel very proud of yourselves." Again, there was a round of applause.

"Third prize goes to Rosemary Kutuz. The second prize goes to Peter Molodtsov. And ... the winner is Maria Katovik. I must say, it was very ingenious of you to think of draping your bike in Russia's national flower, the chamomile."

Amidst much clapping and whistling, the ribbons were handed out and Maria received a tiara and a coupon for a treat at John's Kiosk.

Then came the teenage girls in an egg and spoon contest. I held my breath for them as they made their way carefully across the field. In the end only one of the girls managed successfully, but I couldn't see who it was.

Next Martin announced the tug-of-war and all the teenage boys raced to grab the rope. Before the countdown, Martin reminded them that the winner was the team who won at least two of the three competitions.

When the three-legged race was announced, I quickly grabbed Marg and headed for the starting line. I tied our legs nice and tight and tried to ignore the thrill I felt at being in such close proximity to her. In the next few minutes, I had time to take note of who our opponents were. I was pleasantly surprised to see teams consisting of Marvin and June and beside them Mark and Steve. The last team was Tony and Daria.

Martin called out, "Three, two, one, *go*," while the crowd echoed the countdown.

We were off to a good start, but I could see Marvin and June steadily creeping up on us. Then they were tumbling to the ground, and when someone caught Marg's heel, we too were tumbling beside them. We all fell into a tangled pile about ten yards from the finish line.

I managed to look up in time to witness Mark and Steve crossing the line, inches ahead of Tony and Daria. Marvin and

I were able to untangle ourselves first and reached down to help our partners up, barely able to stand because we were laughing so hard.

The last event was the best outfitted man and woman in traditional dress.

Martin was now saying, "This concludes the competitions. I sure hope you enjoyed your afternoon." While everyone started another round of applause, Martin continued, "A new addition this year is Anna Yusporova, who will be reciting the history of New Petrograd. She has just informed me that Alex's *dedushka* may even join her for a while. We have set a place near the *zakuski* table for her to sit. And now it is time for you all to taste-test the food that everyone has generously brought."

Ignoring the looks Bob and Frank were giving me, Marg and I made our way to where the *zakuski* was set out. After filling our plates, we joined some others sitting at a table.

June had no sooner sat down, her face glowing with excitement, than she asked, "What is this *zakuski* the emcee spoke of?"

Laughing, Marg said, "You just visited it. It refers to a variety of hors d'oeuvres, snacks, appetizers ... usually served buffet style."

"Ah," June said, "that is what we call a potluck."

Bob cleared his throat and I think he was trying to get my attention, but when I ignored him, he turned to Marg instead and inquired, "Did you make these *blini*, Marg? They are delicious, as usual."

Marg, smiling at her brother, replied, "Thank you. They used to be the kids' favorite. Now I see these kids running around with their hotdogs, and I shake my head and think to myself that they don't appreciate fine Russian cuisine. But then, I am fiercely proud of my Russian heritage."

Daria spoke up then to add, "I also brought *blini*, Marg. I hope mine are as good as yours. They were also a family favorite in my household."

"This salad is also enjoyable," June offered. "What did you call it—Olivier salad? It is sure a treat to eat some of your Russian dishes. I've enjoyed myself today immensely. The children with their bikes were the best, though."

I spoke up then and said, "I don't have much recollection of the bicycle contest when I was young, but I sure remember my girls and the excitement in getting their bikes decorated. So much of today has reminded me of family time."

"If you don't mind me asking, how many children do you have, Phil?"

"Not at all. I have twin daughters, Mary Ellen and Marianne. They are now living in Vancouver."

Marg carried on the conversation by saying, "And I have two boys."

This started a heartwarming discussion about our families and in the end, we learned that Marvin and June had two boys and a girl.

As we finished eating, Martin was asking for our attention again by saying, "It is time to announce the winners of today's contests. In the egg-dropping event, I congratulate Alexandra Bolitchn. Come up here to claim your plastic crown. The tug-of-war contest goes to Team Siberia who, as you recall, won all three competitions. Come up and claim your plastic crowns."

To which their captain, Alexander Bolitchn, called out, "We'll pass," which brought a lot of snickers.

"The winners of the very heated three-legged race are Steve Philip and Mark Feodociv."

At this announcement June gave a little gasp and went pale.

When Marvin turned to her with a puzzled expression, I heard June whisper to him, "I will tell you later."

Mark and Steve graciously accepted their plastic crowns and then returned to sit with some of the teenagers. For some reason, it really thrilled me to see that they were building friendships in the village. Martin was now announcing Anna Yusporova and Alex Yusporov as the winners of the best traditional men's and women's dress.

"Your peasant costumes were so charming. Bob has offered as your prize a meal at the Borscht Kettle," to which Alexander Bolitchn yelled out, "Now, that's a prize." This time the crowd laughed out loud.

"And now, one final round of applause for all our competitors. This concludes our day's program. Sit back and enjoy the evening. Of course, as often happens, the field may turn into an impromptu dance floor a little later."

Before anyone else could start a conversation, June quickly asked everyone, "What was the emcee speaking about regarding someone presenting New Petrograd's history? Marvin, don't you think that would be so fascinating? It would be such a special ending to what has been a very wonderful day."

But Marvin replied by saying that he thought his bottle of *tarasun* was making a special ending to a very wonderful day. So, heads shaking, the women all set off to find Anna. I could certainly relate to Marvin because I too was content to settle down with a glass of lingonberry *mors*.

The crowd was beginning to thin after a very happy and full afternoon. I know that when much later, after the dance, as I was walking home, I thought that all this fresh air would help me have a good night's sleep ... that is, if Marg would stay out of my dreams.

CHAPTER TWELVE

Sharlotka Cake

It was good that we had a nice day for Russia Day, because afterwards it turned rainy and windy for a few weeks. I laid low for most of the time in the lighthouse, but when it continued, I eventually wanted to get out for some fresh air. I bundled up and started on my usual route for a walk.

As I was going past the Pagodon place, I saw both Marvin and June in their front garden. I waved a hello and crossed the street to Tony and Daria's.

I think Tony must have seen me coming because when I got to the door, he quickly opened it, saying, "Come in, Phil. It is good to see you on this cold, miserable day."

"Good to see you too, Tony. I was just getting cabin fever—er, lighthouse fever—so decided to ignore the weather and go for a walk."

Tony brought me into their living room, where there was a welcoming fire blazing in the fireplace.

"Sit yourself down and tell me what's new," Tony invited.

Soon we were visiting about everything and nothing. I

must have been there a couple of hours when Daria came in and offered us coffee and a piece of *Sharlotka* cake.

As she was serving us, she mentioned, "I made another cake to take to Marvin and June. What do you think we take a walk across the street and give it to them now?"

"Oh yes, for sure, if you think they'll share?" I said with a smile.

"Really Phil, you've just sat in my house and finished off a piece."

"I agree, Phil," Tony commented, "I wouldn't mind another piece either."

With that, we put on our coats and strode across the street.

Tony knocked on the door and soon June answered and warmly welcomed us in. Daria presented her with the cake, and she quickly invited us to join them for coffee and a piece. We accepted, of course, with a wink between Tony and I.

As June led us down the hall, I caught a glimpse of the boys with their heads down, working on the living room floor. When we arrived in the cozy kitchen, we found Marvin working on a Kinkade lighthouse puzzle. He looked up in surprise to see us all, but quickly invited us to sit down and make ourselves comfortable.

The kitchen soon became a flurry of activity with Marvin putting away his puzzle, Daria cutting the cake and June putting on the coffee. Even I spoke up and asked if there was something I could do. June responded by suggesting that I get the coffee mugs and plates from the cupboard beside the stove. Soon we were all sitting around the table with a coffee mug and piece of cake in front of us.

"Dig in," Marvin suggested, and he soon was exclaiming how delicious the cake was.

June bit into her piece, and then turned to Daria. "Mmm, Marvin's right, this is delicious. You simply must give me the recipe."

"It's just eggs, sugar, sour cream, flour, baking soda and Granny Smith apples. In Russia we called it *Sharlotka*—it's like an apple pie. I'll be happy to write out the recipe for you."

"It sounds like something my mother used to make," June responded.

"Oh, is there Russian background in your family?" I asked.

"Yes, on my mother's side."

And then quickly, as if to change the subject, June said, "It sure is miserable today. Marvin and I were in the garden earlier but we didn't stay out long."

"Yes, much better weather for a puzzle, or entertaining friends," Marvin stated, concluding with a smile for all of us seated around the table.

"Speaking of entertaining," June exclaimed, "we want to plan a potluck next weekend. The floors should be done by then. Marvin and I got to know some folks at Russia Day. We thought that this would help us get to know everyone better. Do you think you could spread the word for us, Daria?"

"Anyone and everyone is welcome," Marvin chimed in.

"I imagine the horseshoe pit is still in the backyard," Tony commented. "In this village, it is a rather important pastime. All us men frequently go to the schoolyard in the evenings and play at a pit there. Do you play, Marvin?"

"Well I didn't play in Vancouver, but I'm having fun tossing a few horseshoes around since I've moved here. It would be nice if the rain stayed away and we could have a game."

"That would be great," I added. "We welcome new competition, even beginners."

"Yes," Tony laughed, "the game is always a challenge and so far this year, Frank is unbeatable."

"How do you like the progress with the floors?" I pried.

"I think it's moving along all right. They are sure making enough noise. They must be doing something," Marvin laughed.

We stayed and chatted a while longer, enjoying the conversation, but as suppertime drew closer we excused ourselves. As I said good night to Tony and Daria, Daria asked if I could stop at the Borscht Kettle and invite Bob and Olga to the potluck.

"No problem," I told her. "I just might stop to pass along the invitation and stay for my dinner."

CHAPTER THIRTEEN

An Invitation

The week went by quickly, with nothing out of the ordinary happening. As I started preparing my contribution for the potluck, I found myself anticipating an enjoyable evening with my neighbours. The more I got to know Marvin and June, the more I anticipated spending time with them. And to think my first impression of June wasn't very favorable. I now knew that she was just a very friendly, bubbly person. I was so pleased to see that we would have nice weather, promising us a pleasant evening.

Marg was waiting at our appointed spot by the shops and it was so pleasant to embrace and hold hands as we strolled along.

"Don't make me spill my *golubtsy,* though," she warned me with a playful growl—at least I hoped it was playful.

I stopped and looked at her in amazement before retorting, "But that's what *I* brought."

We soon joined up with Uri and Anna Golubov and I noticed Anna was pregnant. It flashed through my mind that Bob and Olga were going to be grandparents soon.

"It sure is a lovely summer evening—a rarity here in the Pacific Northwest. I've looked forward to getting together all week," I said in greeting to everyone.

Anna quickly turned towards us, exclaiming, "Well, Aunty Marg, isn't this a special new occurrence? Papa has told me about it," as she hugged and kissed Marg on the cheek.

"Where's mine?" I couldn't resist asking.

"Oh, Uncle Phil," she said as she laughingly wrapped me in a huge bear hug.

"What about you, my dear?" Marg was saying. "It looks like you and my handsome nephew-in-law have some news to share as well."

"I've been telling her she can't hide it any longer, especially after tonight," Uri responded, giving his wife a smooch.

Soon we joined up with John and Katarina Molodtsov with their children Maria and Peter. I heard someone mention that Father Nikolas was coming with Frank and Betty.

June greeted us at the door, then rushed away and I heard her calling out, "Marvin, do you have the charcoal on?"

"Sure do," Marvin said. "I need help right now setting up the buffet table and the chairs."

"Be right there," Bob and I called back.

As Bob and I were setting up the table, Bob squeezed my arm and said, "It sure is nice to see you officially with my sister. I've hoped something like this would happen for a long time, a very long time. Not saying I didn't enjoy having Merle in the family."

Soon a nice group of the village folk were gathered and June announced that everything was ready. We all grabbed a chair and Father Nikolas said grace. The children were soon all gathered around Marvin, eagerly anticipating a hotdog or hamburger. I grabbed Marg's hand and headed to join the food line at the table.

"This is some potluck you are having. Thank you for inviting everyone. The village folk really don't get together enough," I remarked to June.

It felt so good for Marg and me to head back together with our plates of food to some chairs with no inquiring eyes on us.

"June, what did you call this salad you made?" Olga asked.

"It is a potato salad and so simple to make," June replied. "Just boil a few potatoes, add in green onions and grated carrot, mix with mayonnaise and it's ready."

"Did I hear you tell someone that you made a chocolate mousse cheesecake?" Marvin inquired.

"Yes," June said, with a knowing smile. "Daria, did you make some more of the *blini* that you brought to Russia Day?"

"No, I didn't. I thought I would make an Italian dish Tony likes. I think Anna brought the *blini*."

"Yes, I did bring it. Everything is all so good and such a variety of dishes—Russian, Italian, Canadian," Anna replied.

"Yes, that is just what I was thinking," Marg agreed.

"Anna, I see that you may have some news to share," Katarina commented.

"Told you so," Uri said, as he smiled at his wife, before Anna answered.

"Our baby will be due in late November. We are hiring a midwife to come here to help with the delivery."

Olga quickly responded to her. "Don't be too brave, Anna, honey. This is your first baby, and uh, sometimes they do cause difficulties. A trip to Vancouver can easily be arranged."

"Yes," Betty added, with a knowing look to Olga. "If the District Nurse isn't available to make the arrangements, please give me a call. We can sure make them."

I was just finishing my desserts of cheesecake and *Kissel* when Marvin called out, "Who is up for horseshoes?" and I headed to the pit.

Several of the children were clamouring around Marvin asking if they could try. I smiled to myself, thinking that they sure must have enjoyed those hotdogs and hamburgers. Marvin was now their new best friend.

It didn't take long until the children lost interest in horseshoes and began a rowdy game with their water pistols, chasing each other around the yard. I heard Marg shriek from where the ladies were all sitting, and Katarina calling, "Peter Roman!"

The incident seemed to start a mass exodus of all the families leaving to go home.

"Whew," I said as I sat down with a drink of *medovukha*, "those were some serious games of horseshoes tonight, and still Frank is defending his title!"

"Frank just lives too close to the horseshoe pit by the schoolyard," Uri laughed in response to my statement. "I see him there all the time."

Evening was really starting to close in and it was getting dark outside when June remarked, "I would invite you all inside for coffee and what is left of the desserts, but our floors still aren't finished."

Immediately I felt alert and Tony asked if he could take a look.

"Sure," Marvin answered, and we all traipsed inside to the living room. I was just going through the kitchen door when I heard Tony, who was ahead of me, let out a string of Italian. I hurried my steps.

"Ooh," Daria said from behind me, "that doesn't sound good. He only does that when he is really upset."

Tony was remarking to everyone gathered in the room, "I

really don't know what they are doing in here. It looks like they are ripping all the floorboards up, even to the diagonally laid tongue-and-groove sub-flooring. However, it appears they are not putting the new flooring down. I think we need to chat with these boys. Phil, Bob, Frank—could you help me with that tomorrow morning?

"Marvin, what time do they usually get here?" I asked.

"I serve them coffee and toast at eight in the morning," June replied. "It starts their day out right."

"What do you say, fellows? Can you meet me at my place around then?" Tony asked.

Bob said "For sure," but Frank felt he needed to get the store open.

"Well," I said, "I'll be here for sure. I am most anxious to hear what they have to say."

With plans arranged to confront Mark and Steve in the morning, we set out for our respective homes. The night had turned very dark and windy, but I wasn't sure which was the darkest, the night or my thoughts as I walked Marg home and then trudged back to the lighthouse.

CHAPTER FOURTEEN

Confrontation

I woke up and rolled over in bed, reflecting about the lovely evening we'd had at Marvin and June's. Then I remembered the plans we had made last night and hurried to get ready to join Bob and Tony.

I wandered over to the Borscht Kettle for breakfast. Bob served us a nice hearty breakfast of sausages, eggs and toast. We sipped our coffee and discussed the task at hand.

"Maybe we should get going," I urged. "Tony will be waiting for us at his place."

"Well, we have to wait for Olga to take over before I can leave. She shouldn't be long," Bob stated.

Soon we saw Olga turning the corner and heading in our direction.

When she came in, Bob said to her, "We shouldn't be long. Do you think you could have sandwiches for seven for lunch? I imagine everyone will be with us when we come back." And then we were on our way to Tony's.

It was half past nine when we knocked on the door. June

answered and hustled us in. We could hear the sound of Mark and Steve talking in the other room as we sat in the kitchen.

"What do you think of us confronting Mark and Steve on their work?" Tony said.

"Well, I really don't want a big confrontation. What do you think, June?" Marvin asked.

"Well, honey, I agree with Tony that we should speak to them. At least ask them to give us a progress report. Shall I invite them to join us for coffee?" June walked towards the door and called into the living room, "Guys, I know it is a little earlier than usual, but what about a coffee break?"

Mark and Steve set down their tools and followed June back into the room.

I think I saw Steve kind of stiffen when he walked into the room and saw us all sitting here. It was so subtle that I wasn't sure if it happened, because then he was back to his usual cordial self, greeting us all.

June poured them coffee, and offered them a piece of cheesecake left over from the potluck.

Tony looked uneasy, but finally said, "You know June and Marvin graciously hosted a potluck last night. I'm sure you heard them talking about it as you worked here during the week. At the end of the evening, when June mentioned she couldn't invite us in because the floors weren't finished, I asked to see how the job was going. I guess because of my long years doing renovation jobs, a job always interests me. I was shocked, though, to see how slowly this project is progressing. I would have thought that the flooring would be down by now and you would have begun the next stage of the renovations. It seems all you have done is to rip up the old flooring."

Steve responded, "Well, we haven't actually done too many jobs laying hardwood, so I guess we aren't as fast as others."

Mark then interjected, "What we are really doing is—"

"Mark!" Steve shouted.

The room fell silent as everyone looked at Mark and Steve. In just a few minutes it seemed to grow tenser as the two men stared at each other.

Bob finally put on his sheriff's hat, looked at them and said, "These actions are getting more questionable. Steve, why did just you interrupt Mark?"

Steve's face turned very red, and he wouldn't even look up.

Bob said to Mark and Steve, "If you boys can't explain what is going on here... As far as I can tell, you haven't done anything illegal, but I have the feeling that it would be in everyone's best interests if you just quietly sailed on out of our village."

In what seemed like an impulsive statement, June spoke up, "You boys wouldn't be looking for something hidden, would you?"

I turned from June and noticed how pale they went. I sure didn't understand June's comment, but I was quite sure that it had an effect on the boys.

Bob spoke then to the others in the room. "Tony, would you mind getting Daria and meeting us at the Borscht Kettle in half an hour?"

Then Bob took hold of Steve's arm and motioned for me to take hold of Mark. We escorted them down Marine Street to the dock where their boat was moored. The boys, working in a daze, slowly took time to get their gear ready, but soon their little boat was ready to go.

I must admit that I had mixed feelings watching their boat glide past the craggy point and out of sight.

We turned and then headed back to the Borscht Kettle. I must say the sandwich and coffee Olga prepared sure went down easy. Just being together with Bob was helping me to unwind from the morning's events. Soon the others came by, except June and Marvin weren't with them.

In answer to my question, Tony said, "They will be along shortly. It seems they had to do something in their garden."

We were just finishing our lunch when they appeared. Olga quickly brought out more sandwiches and coffee.

It seemed the morning had left us void of any conversation, but I had to ask June, "What was that comment that you made to Mark and Steve about searching for something?"

"Yes, I was just going to tell everyone, but before I begin, I have to say that I can't help but feel badly about what happened this morning. As I had mentioned before, we have three adult children, and, well, I guess Mark and Steve just seemed like sons to me."

"Before you start, June," Marvin said, "I would like to thank you all for rallying around June and me considering that we are new to your village. And Tony, I am hoping that we can discuss later you taking over the project."

"I second that," June agreed. "I admit that I was sad to see them go, but I sure appreciate everyone's help."

CHAPTER FIFTEEN

June Speaks

The question was burning within me, when finally June began to answer.

"This is a story of my family ... *babushka* Elena Bolitchnova and Great Aunt Tatyana Feodociv. They were working as confidantes in the Russian court before the revolution. Tensions were high in Mother Russia and the royal family felt it best to send several of their employees out of the country with royal jewels. They hid them by sewing the jewels into their undergarments, or in the hems of their clothing. Some of the men had jewels sewn into the linings of their hats.

"Many of these people were caught and killed leaving Mother Russia. Sadly, my *dedushka* Bolitchnov was one of the people killed, so I never knew him. Great Aunt Tatyana and *babushka* Elena with baby Margarita made it out safely to London, where they sailed to the new world, and a new life in this seemingly strange land. Baby Margarita Molotz was my mother. On the ship coming over, Great Aunt Tatyana met and fell in love with Yaroslav Pagodonov."

A collective murmur went up in the room.

"Some of our founding fathers," June continued, "were married soon after they landed in Halifax. Then Great Aunt Tatyana and her new husband traveled west to New Petrograd to start their life as a married couple. I believe they had a very happy life here with the other Russians who had fled Mother Russia, but they were never blessed with children.

"When my great aunt was near death, she confided in my mother, who was by then her only living relative, about the jewels she had escaped with, hidden in her coat.

"I might add that I was quite shocked to learn Mark's last name at Russia Day, because it was the same name as my great aunt. It made me wonder if he was a distant relative that we didn't know about."

"I seem to remember that you gave little gasp when you heard his name," I said.

But June just continued on. "We know from history that all of the Russian royal family was shot and so she and her husband kept the jewels themselves. These jewels were hidden in their home. I think back to our evening with Anna Yusporova and the question about how they paid for the journey and the boats, and I wondered how many other jewels might be hidden in New Petrograd. That was the only information my mother got, and then my great aunt was not able to communicate any more.

"So, through the years, I kept watching for this house to go on the market and when it did, we purchased it for our retirement. Since moving in, I too have been on the search for the jewels. One day I came home with my arms laden with wild flowers and was going in the front door, when I caught a glimpse of something sparkling in the doorknob. I went back later to investigate, never expecting the Russian jewels, but there they were. Once disturbed, they all came tumbling out. My hands couldn't catch them all and some spilled onto the verandah. They had been hidden for I can only guess how many years behind a trap door in the front door knob.

"I buried them in the garden until I received confirmation from my lawyer that yes, indeed, they would be ours, as the last living descendant of my Great Aunt Tatyana. I have since dug them up and Marvin and I have found a much safer place for the jewels until we decide what to do."

"Hmph," Olga said, "that probably explains why the Pagodons always seemed to have money to do what they wanted ... like build the biggest house in New Petrograd."

"Wasn't it them who built the original church and schoolhouse?" Daria asked.

Such babble erupted when June finished telling her story.

Everyone asked so many questions, but the only one June did answer was, "What became of your mother and *babushka*?"

June started by saying, "Thank you for asking that question. My *babushka* and mother moved to just outside of Halifax in a town called Truro. My *babushka* managed to take a job as a housekeeper to a local dairy farmer, a very kind gentleman named Mr. Harris.

"In 1920, Russia's Grand Duchess Olga Alexandrovna Romanov, her husband Nikolai Kulikovsky, and two sons fled post-revolution Russia for Denmark. In Denmark, the family farmed. In 1948, again feeling threatened, they emigrated to Ontario. My *babushka* and mother also came west at the same time, similarly settling in Ontario. I do not know if my *babushka* was hoping to become a confidante again, but in Canada the duchess led a very simple life. My family eventually settled in Fort Erie. So I was raised in eastern Canada, coming west in my twenties, where I met Marvin."

June fell silent then, and for every other question, her answer was just to smile.

It was still early afternoon when I went back to the lighthouse, but this day had drained me. It seemed one of the longest days that I could remember. Maybe tonight I would just wander over to Marg's in time for one of her home-cooked meals and an evening of relaxing conversation. I was sure she would be waiting to hear about the events of the day.

THE END

GLOSSARY

Daria approached June one day and said, "How would you like to learn the definitions of some Russian foods?"

June didn't hesitate. "That would be delightful. Going around town, and in Frank and Betty's store, I have heard so many mentioned. I wondered what they were."

"Let's start by going to the Borscht Kettle and looking at one of Bob's menus."

Along the way, they met Anna Golubova who, when they told her where they were going, decided to go along. "*Papa*—Dad—will love getting in on this conversation," she said.

At the Borscht Kettle, they saw that the Daily Special was *beef stroganoff*.

June spoke first. "I didn't know that was a Russian dish. I'm pretty familiar with taking a piece of beef and cutting it into little strips and mixing it in sour cream."

"Only we call sour cream *smetana*," Anne and Daria answered her in unison.

Then Daria pointed at the menu. "Was the dish you so enjoyed at Russia Day *blini*?"

"Yes, those delicious little pancakes," June said enthusiastically. "They were so good. Someone brought them to our place the night of the potluck, too."

Daria said, "To give you a few more details, *blini* is sometimes called *blin*. You're right—it is a Russian pancake. Traditionally we make it from wheat or buckwheat flour, then top it with sour cream, butter, and other garnishes you may have in your fridge."

"People also call them blintzes, crepes or *palatschinke*. My *babushka*—" Anna turned to June with a smile. "My grandmother made the best *blini* ever."

Bob came alongside the table. "Remember that evening when we first met Mark and Steve and I told them about *coulibiac*?"

June, smiling in greeting, said, "Yes, and if I recall correctly, you said it was a fish loaf made of salmon with rice, hard-boiled eggs, mushrooms, and dill."

"Very good," Daria said with approval. "Traditionally they may have used sturgeon instead of salmon. I always remember *dedushka*—grandfather—loved this dish. He was always asking us to make it."

"June, do you remember," Anna added, "the dish Phil and Aunty Marg brought to your place for the potluck?"

"Yes, I do," June responded. "What was it called—*golubtsy*? It was just cooked cabbage leaves wrapped around a variety of fillings."

"You have a good memory!" Daria said. "Then to end a meal you can make *Kissel*. That's a fruit dessert of sweetened juice, thickened with arrowroot, cornstarch or even potato starch."

June nodded. "After everyone left, Marvin kept talking about how much he enjoyed it."

Anna spoke up. "This is thirsty work. I think I would like some *kvass*."

"What is that?" June asked.

Olga, who had just come in, answered, "That's a fermented, non-alcoholic drink made from black or regular rye bread or dough."

"Hi *Mama*, I mean, mother," Anna said. "We're teaching June some Russian. Could I please have a *mors*?"

In response to June's questioning look, Daria spoke up. "Don't worry. That's just a non-carbonated Russian fruit drink we make from berries. It can be made from lots of varieties, but traditionally from lingonberry and cranberries. Sometimes blueberries, strawberries or raspberries, depending on what we grow in the short season here—or what Frank can order."

June said, "Please tell me more about Olivier Salad."

"For sure." Olga joined them at the table. "It really is just another version of potato salad. So of course, we start with diced potatoes, eggs, chicken or bologna, sweet peas and pickles with a mayonnaise dressing. You can add other vegetables, too, such as carrot or fresh cucumbers."

Daria, laughing, said, "I just check my fridge to see what I have on hand. Another dessert is—"

Before she could go any further, Anna said, "*Papa*—Dad—can you bring us all a piece of Sharlotka cake?"

"Of course," Bob said. "My treat. Did you know it was invented in London in the nineteenth century by a French cook by the name of Marie Antoine Careme? The Russian part came when it was served to Tsar Alexander I. In the beginning they called it *Charlotte à la Parisienne*. Later on, the dessert was renamed *Charlotte Russe* and it became famous all over the world."

As they sat enjoying their cake, Daria said, "June, maybe that is enough food to learn about for one day."

June responded, "Yes, I'm getting pretty saturated with all these facts. But I do want to ask about a few drinks I've heard mentioned."

"Sure, which ones?"

The door opened again and in came Marvin, Phil, Tony and Uri, all disheveled and grass-stained. Two of them conveniently ordered glasses of *medovukha*.

"That's a traditional Russian honey-based drink—you know, like mead," Daria said. "Tony's drinking a *tarasun*, which looks clear, but it packs a punch—it's fermented mare's milk. Tony calls it 'milk whisky'."

"Oh-oh," June said. "You'd better tell me what Marvin's drinking."

"That's *stewle*. It's a fermented milk product like *ryazhenka*, but it's made by adding *smetana* to baked milk."

"Well," Bob concluded, looking around him, "it looks like the gang's all here. How about staying to finish off the beef stroganoff?"

Amidst several affirmatives, Phil responded, "What, no *zakuski* tonight?"

Daria whispered to June, "Remember? That means a variety of hors d'oeuvres, snacks, appetizers, usually served buffet style. I've seen cold cuts, cured fish, mixed salads, *kholodets*, various pickled vegetables and mushrooms, *pirozhki*, caviar, deviled eggs, open sandwiches, canapés and breads."

Bob and Olga hastened to serve their guests, and when they finished, sat down with a plate of beef stroganoff to join the merry party. Anna raised her voice and declared, "My *rhoditeli*—my parents—are the best!"

Part Two

RECIPES

BLINI (RUSSIAN CREPES)

"June, how about I teach you to prepare some of the Russian dishes you have enjoyed at Russia Day and at the potluck you and Marvin hosted in your home?" Daria asked. "I think the first dish to start with is blini."

June responded, "That would be perfect—Marvin will be joining the men for a game of horseshoes on Saturday morning. I would also like to learn about Olivier Salad, Holiday Cranberry Kissel, and Sharlotka Cake. Can we do those, too?"

Ingredients

- 2/3 cup all-purpose flour
- 1/2 cup buckwheat flour
- 1/2 teaspoon salt
- 1 teaspoon yeast (instant or rapid-rise)
- 1 cup warm milk
- 2 tablespoons melted butter

- 1 large egg (room temperature, separated)
- Garnish of choice

Instructions

Take a large bowl and mix all the dry ingredients together. Next you will want to make a well in the center. Pour the warm milk into the well, and mix it up until the batter is smooth. Cover it up and let it rise until it is doubled, which will take approximately an hour. (A good time to clean up the kitchen!)

Melt the butter and when it cools off a little, stir it into the batter. Next, separate the egg white from the egg yolk. Set the white aside and add the egg yolk into the batter. In a separate bowl, whisk the egg white until it's stiff but not so dry that it forms cracks. Fold the egg white into the batter and then cover. Let this mixture stand for 20 minutes.

Turn on an element to medium heat and put on a non-stick skillet to heat it up. Drop quarter-size dollops of dough into the pan, allowing a lot of room between each blini. Cook for about 1 minute or until bubbles form on top and then turn them over. After turning, cook for another 30 seconds more. Cover the blini and keep warm until your meal is ready. Repeat Step 4 until all the batter is used up, and serve with Daria's garnishes.

> "I have a few suggestions on how to serve the blini," Daria said. "These have been passed down to us. You can use red or black caviar, smoked salmon or other fish, chopped hard-cooked eggs, minced red or white onion, sour cream or crème fraîche, chopped dill, and lemon wedges."

OLIVIER SALAD

Daria said, “Like most potato salads, Olivier Salad is made ahead of time. Sometimes I chop all the ingredients and store them in the refrigerator. I then mix them together and add the mayonnaise a few hours before serving. This way, you will have your preparation done a few days before you plan to use it.”

June was thrilled to learn Olivier Salad was very much like the potato salad she made for the potluck, just with a few different ingredients.

Ingredients

- 3 small or medium potatoes
- 4 medium carrots
- 8 eggs, hard boiled
- 1 pound bologna
- 8 small pickles
- 1–2 small cucumbers
- 1 can (14–15 oz) peas

- 1½ cups mayonnaise
- Optional: 1 small onion or fresh chives

Instructions

Start by boiling the potatoes and the carrots in their skins ("The vitamins under the skins are good for you, Anna says," Daria told June) in a medium pot just until tender, or about 20-30 minutes, depending on the size of the vegetables. ("Anna also told me I should cut the carrots into smaller pieces than the potatoes so they will cook more evenly," Daria said. "Don't overcook them—nobody likes a mushy salad!")

Hard-boil your eggs, and when cool, peel them and set them aside to cool completely.

Open the can of peas and drain them well.

Dice the potatoes, carrots, eggs, pickles and cucumbers, if you're using them, into quarter-inch pieces. Chop the bologna into the same size pieces.

If you're using onions, mince them fine (chives or green onions are very nice to use if you have them in your fridge).

Mix up all the ingredients with the mayonnaise. Serves 8–10.

HOLIDAY CRANBERRY KISSEL

"I love Kissel," Daria said to June. "I love how velvety and custardy it is. Did you know that Russians have been making it since the twelfth century?"

"There were things in the cupboards when we bought the house that might have been that old," June said.

"Well, around here we use cranberries, cherries, and red currants. Sometimes apples, if I make it in the winter. Come on, I'll show you."

Ingredients

- 2 large apples, diced small, enough to make 2 cups
- 1½ cups fresh cranberries
- 1¼ cups filtered water
- ½ cup honey, or more to taste
- ¼ cup organic corn or potato starch
- ¼ teaspoon cinnamon
- 1 cup fresh whipping cream, whipped

Instructions

Place the first three ingredients in a pan and bring to a boil. Then simmer for 10 minutes. After taking off the burner, set aside to cool a little.

Blend until smooth in texture. (Traditionally this was done by forcing the mixture through a sieve. But nowadays most of us have a blender or Cuisinart to help us.)

Add the next three ingredients—honey, starch and cinnamon—and mix them together slightly. Do not overmix. Return to the pan and simmer for 2–3 minutes until the mixture thickens up.

Take the pan off the heat and place it in a bowl of ice water to cool it quickly. Then stir the mixture, using a whisk.

Fold in whipped cream until soft peaks form.

Cover and refrigerate. Serves 12.

Daria told June, "You can fix Kissel without the whipped cream folded in. When you're ready to serve it, put the whipped cream on the top with a mint leaf as garnish. Or, you can serve it vegan style, without whipped cream. Tony loves soy whipped cream, so sometimes I use that for a substitute."

SHARLOTKA CAKE

"You probably know this one by its French name," Daria said as she put June to slicing the apples. "Some people call it Charlotte Russe."

Ingredients

- 6 eggs
- 1 cup sugar
- ¼ cup sour cream
- ¾ teaspoon baking soda, dissolved in ½ teaspoon vinegar
- 4 large Granny Smith or other tart apples

Preparation

Start by preheating the oven to 350 degrees.

Take a round cake pan and grease and flour it. Cut parchment paper to fit the bottom of your cake pan and line it. ("It's easier to use baking spray instead of the butter or oil and flour," Daria said. "But remember to spray the top of the parchment paper as well.")

Instructions

Next, whisk together the eggs and sugar until they are pale yellow and foamy. Add in the sour cream to the mixture.

Dissolve the baking soda in vinegar and then add that to the batter also. Mix to combine.

Add the flour to the batter and mix just until the flour is mixed in. Do not overmix this step.

Meanwhile, core and peel the apples and cut into small, thin slices. Layer the apples decoratively in the bottom of the prepared cake pan. Pour the batter over the apples and distribute it evenly.

Place in the oven on the centre rack and bake for 45–50 minutes, until the cake is a golden brown. A toothpick inserted into the cake's center will come out clean when it is ready.

Run a spatula or butter knife around the edges of the cake pan to loosen it, then flip the cake over onto a cooling rack. The parchment paper will just peel right off the cake.

To serve the cake, flip it back over so it is apple side up. Allow it to cool for about 15 minutes and then serve. Serves 8.

"As a final step," Daria suggested as June managed to flip the cake the second time, "we can dust it with confectioner's sugar and cinnamon. Look, it came out beautifully!"

AFTERWORD

This book was written by three residents of Carewest Garrison Green long-term care facility, in Calgary, Alberta, Canada.

The group would get together once a week to "write the book." One member would throw out an idea, and the others would discuss, change it, or decide it wasn't quite right.

In the beginning the book didn't have a focus, but then one evening an idea was thrown out that caused Diana to speak about the Russian royal family at the time of the Russian Revolution in 1917. She mentioned the Russian royal family smuggling jewels, which brought about a search on the Internet to find some article that substantiated that information. From then the book had a focal point. This required revisiting some earlier chapters to make sure they gelled with the later chapters. Adding a love interest to Phil's life, well, just added a touch of romance.

We had loads of fun writing *Lighthouse in the Mist* and we hope you have had just as much pleasure reading it.

Made in the USA
San Bernardino, CA
23 December 2018